The Brav Horse Brothers

and other horse stories

Compiled by Vic Parker

Miles
Kelly

First published in 2014 by Miles Kelly Publishing Ltd
Harding's Barn, Bardfield End Green, Thaxted, Essex, CM6 3PX, UK

2 4 6 8 10 9 7 5 3 1

Publishing Director Belinda Gallagher
Creative Director Jo Cowan
Editorial Director Rosie Neave
Senior Editor Claire Philip
Designer Rob Hale
Production Manager Elizabeth Collins
Reprographics Stephan Davis, Jennifer Hunt, Thom Allaway

ISBN 978-1-78209-653-5

Printed in China

British Library Cataloguing-in-Publication Data
A catalogue record for this book is available from the British Library

ACKNOWLEDGEMENTS
The publishers would like to thank the following artists who have contributed to this book:
Advocate Art: Simon Mendez (Cover)
The Bright Agency: Mélanie Florian and Kirsteen Harris-Jones (inc. borders)
Frank Endersby

Made with paper from a sustainable forest

www.mileskelly.net
info@mileskelly.net

Contents

Griffen, the High Flyer

By James Baldwin

The winged horse in this story is a descendant of Pegasus who, according to Greek mythology, carried thunderbolts for the great god Zeus.

OLD ATLANTES, THE WIZARD of the Pyrenees, built a tower for his laboratory on the topmost peak of a grey mountain. He built it with solid walls, a single narrow door, and a dome of glass at the top. By night, he sat in the dome and gazed at the stars. By day, he sat inside the tower surrounded by his magic circles and books and pots and vials and herbs. Sometimes the people in the valley below saw thick clouds of black smoke coming out of the chimney of the wizard's den and even reported that they had seen sheets of flame and balls of red fire shooting out from the high tower.

Everyone in the nearby countryside feared Atlantes, but he didn't care as long as they did not disturb him in his studies and experiments. He was searching for the secret of how to make the magical philosopher's stone, with which he would be able to turn anything into gold.

Atlantes thought that he knew how to make it, if only he could get a vial of lightning…

One night, when a great storm was raging in the mountains, and the thunder was rolling from peak to peak, and flashes of lightning filled the air with terror, Atlantes tried an experiment. He left his tower and went to a cave in the side of the mountain, where he placed a huge jar and several pots of magic ingredients. He arranged them very carefully, and went back to his tower to wait.

In the morning, when the storm had cleared away, the wizard hurried to the cave. To his amazement there sprang from the huge jar a white horse with great wings that reflected all of the colours of the rainbow. Atlantes thought he must look very like Pegasus, the mythical horse. He called the horse Griffen and the airy creature became his.

Now the wizard, with the aid of his winged steed, built himself an even more marvellous castle of magic, with shining walls and lofty turrets. The local people were stunned to look up and see it among the mountaintops, but even more amazed to see a horse flying in mid-air with the white-bearded wizard seated on its back.

Every morning, with his great spectacles astride his nose and a great big book in his hands, Atlantes would mount his winged horse and soar out over the countryside to some spot where a noble knight or a fair maiden would be likely to be passing during the day.

He would wait until his unsuspecting victim drew near, then the horse would suddenly swoop down and block the road. Then Atlantes would read aloud from his book and the traveller would forget everything, come meekly forwards, allowing themselves to be lifted up behind the wizard and carried aloft on Griffen back to the magic castle, to keep Atlantes company there forever.

Time passed, and so many people went missing from the surrounding lands that a brave young man called Astolpho made up his mind to find the castle and defeat the

wizard. He rode a beautiful black horse named Rabican, which was so sure-footed it could climb where no other horse could.

So Astolpho on Rabican made his way high up the mountain and finally reached the entrance to the great white castle. The gate was open, as if beckoning him to enter. Astolpho urged Rabican forwards into a courtyard with shady trees and fountains. Knights and ladies were there playing chess, but they took no notice of him.

All at once, an old man with a long flowing beard came out of the castle and began to read. But Astolpho too had a book, a book given to him by an Indian prince, which contained spells against all enchantments.

Without heeding the wizard he looked in this book to see how he might escape, and found the right instruction:

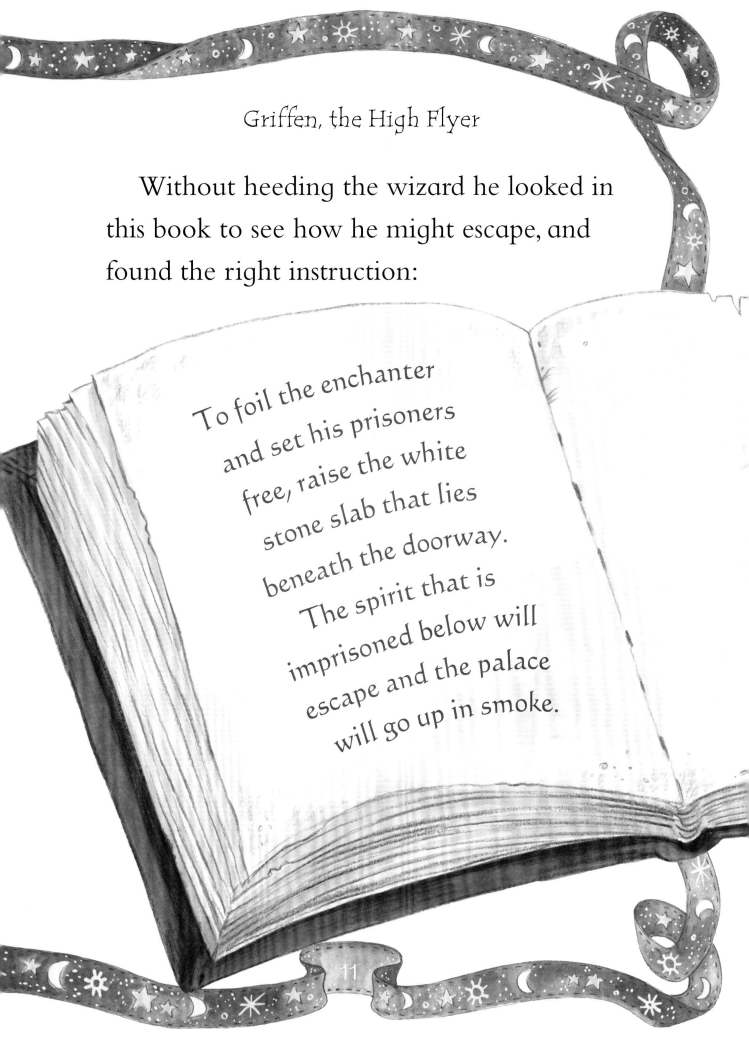

To foil the enchanter and set his prisoners free, raise the white stone slab that lies beneath the doorway. The spirit that is imprisoned below will escape and the palace will go up in smoke.

While the wizard was still trying to complete the words of his spell, Astolpho slid from Rabican's back, ran to the doorway, found the white stone, and prised it up with his spear. There, before him, was a spacious chamber. Griffen was inside, saddled and bridled and ready for flight. Astolpho lost no time in springing onto his back and soaring up into the air.

With a clap of thunder, the palace of enchantment disappeared, leaving the knights and ladies standing

dazed on the mountainside.
One by one, they awoke from
the spells placed upon them,
and began following
Rabican down the steep
path that led back to their
homelands.

As for Griffen and
Astolpho, they proudly
swooped off to have
adventures all over the
world – even once
flying up to the moon!

Jupiter
and the
Horse

By Gotthold Ephraim Lessing

This story is taken from a collection of fables written by a German man in 1759. It features a horse and the chief god in Roman mythology, Jupiter.

ONE DAY, the horse boldly approached the throne of Jupiter and said, "Father of all humans and creatures, everyone agrees that I am one of the most beautiful animals that you created to bless the world

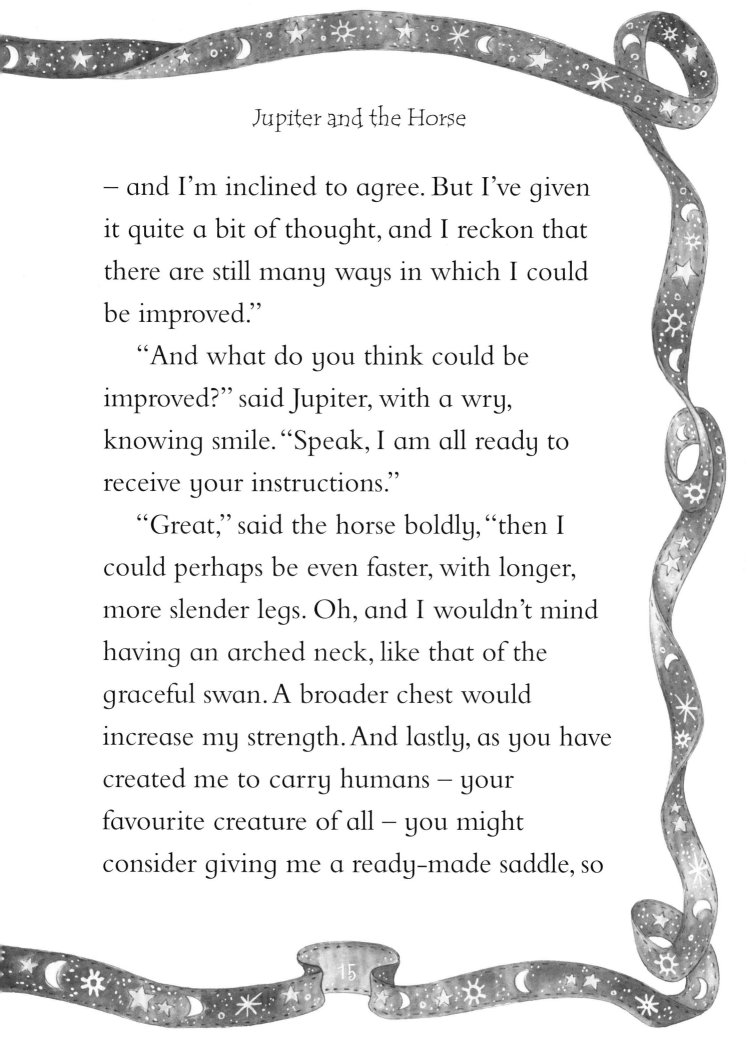

– and I'm inclined to agree. But I've given it quite a bit of thought, and I reckon that there are still many ways in which I could be improved."

"And what do you think could be improved?" said Jupiter, with a wry, knowing smile. "Speak, I am all ready to receive your instructions."

"Great," said the horse boldly, "then I could perhaps be even faster, with longer, more slender legs. Oh, and I wouldn't mind having an arched neck, like that of the graceful swan. A broader chest would increase my strength. And lastly, as you have created me to carry humans – your favourite creature of all – you might consider giving me a ready-made saddle, so people don't have to use their own."

"Well then," said Jupiter, "wait just a moment." His face became very thoughtful and serious and, holding up his hands, he spoke the magic words of creation.

A cloud of dust blew up from the ground. It whirled into a huge shape, grew solid and then began to move. And suddenly in front of his throne there stood – the awkward and clumsy camel!

The horse stared at the new creature from its head to its toes and gave a shudder of disgust.

"So, here are the longer, slimmer legs," explained Jupiter. "And look, it has an arched neck, a broader chest and a useful saddle. So shall I make you look like this?"

Jupiter and the Horse

The horse, all aquiver with fear, dared not say anything to Jupiter, and stayed very quiet indeed.

"I should think so too," said Jupiter firmly. "Go on your way then – I won't punish you as long as you have learned your lesson. But I shall leave this new creature just as he is, to remind you of how

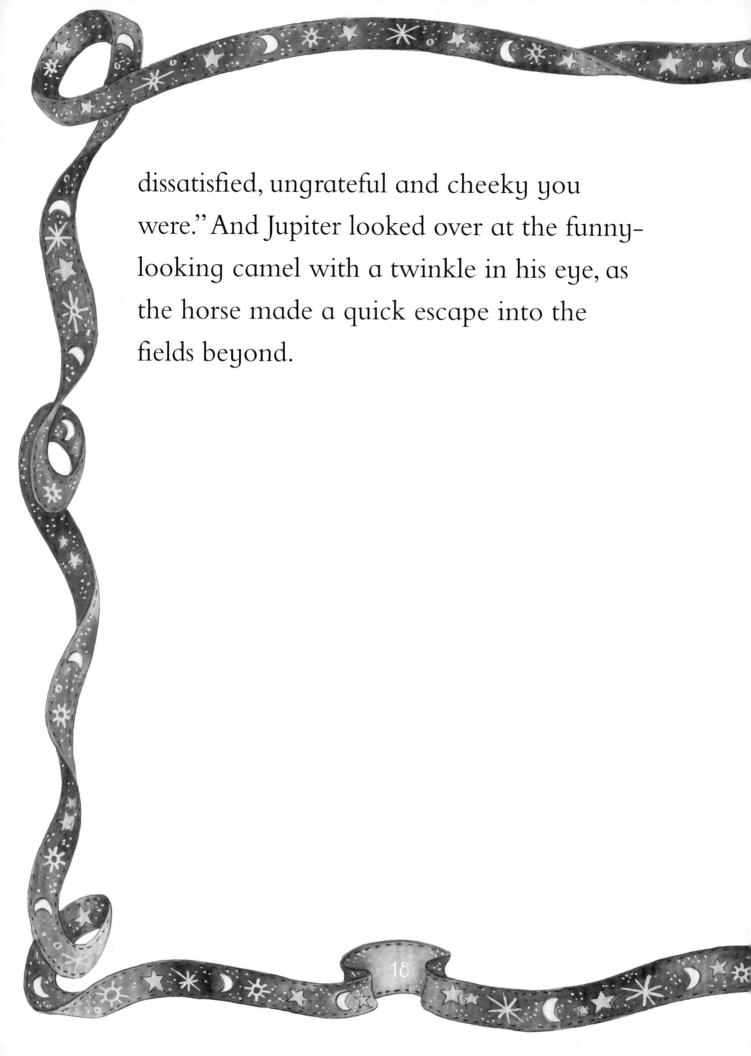

dissatisfied, ungrateful and cheeky you were." And Jupiter looked over at the funny-looking camel with a twinkle in his eye, as the horse made a quick escape into the fields beyond.

The Giant
and the
Unicorn

A retelling of a traditional Jewish
folktale by Gertrude Landa

ALL THE ANIMALS gathered in front
of the Ark and began to march
forwards into it, while Father Noah
carefully inspected them. He seemed very
troubled indeed. "I wonder," he said to
himself, "how I shall obtain a unicorn,

and how I shall get it into the Ark."

"I can bring you a unicorn, Father Noah," he heard in a booming voice of thunder, and turning round he saw the giant, Og. "But you must agree to save me from the flood as well."

"Go away," cried Noah. "You are not an animal – giants aren't allowed on the Ark."

"Please pity me," whined the giant to Noah. "See how I am shrinking. Once I was so tall that I could drink water from the clouds and warm my face at the sun. I fear not that I shall be drowned, but that all the food will be destroyed and that I shall perish of hunger."

Noah refused once more and Og wandered off. But he was soon back, bringing with him a unicorn.

It was huge, although the giant said it was the smallest he could find. It lay down in front of the Ark, and for some time Noah was puzzled about what to do, until at last a bright idea struck him. He attached the huge beast to the Ark by a rope fastened to its horn so that it could swim alongside them and be fed.

Og seated himself on a mountain nearby and watched the rain pouring down. It fell faster and faster in torrents until the rivers overflowed and the waters began to rise rapidly on the land and sweep all things away. Father Noah stood gloomily before the door of the Ark until the water reached his neck. Then it swept him inside. The door closed with a bang, and the Ark rose gallantly on the flood and began to move along. The unicorn swam alongside and, as it passed Og, the giant jumped nimbly onto its back.

"See, Father Noah," he cried, with a huge chuckle, "you will have to save me after all, or I will snatch all the food you put through the window for the unicorn."

Noah saw that it was useless to argue with Og, who might easily, indeed, sink the Ark with his tremendous strength.

"I will make a bargain with you," Noah shouted from a window. "I will feed you, but you must promise to be a servant for me and my family when the flood is over."

Og was very hungry, so he accepted the

conditions and devoured his first breakfast.

The rain continued to fall in great big sheets that shut out the light of day. Inside the Ark, however, all was bright and cheerful, for Noah had placed precious stones in the windows.

One day the rain ceased, the clouds rolled away and the sun shone brilliantly again. How strange the world looked! It was like a vast ocean. Nothing but water could be seen anywhere, and only one or two of the highest mountain-tops peeped above the flood. All the world was drowned, and Noah gazed on the desolate scene from one of the windows with tears in his eyes.

Finally, after sailing for days and days some land appeared and the Ark rested on

Mount Ararat. Og sat nearby on the hillside and watched the animals leave the Ark and spread out over the land. Finally Noah set loose the mighty unicorn and it galloped away and disappeared from sight.

Then Noah's children began to build houses – and Og had to labour as their servant. Daily he complained that he was shrinking to the size of the mortals, for Noah said there was not enough food for him to keep his size.

And that is how giants came to be no different from humans and how the unicorn became the rarest beast of all.

The Brave Horse Brothers

A version of an ancient Romanian
folktale by Andrew Lang

ONCE UPON A TIME there lived an
emperor who was a great conqueror,
and he reigned over many countries.
Whenever he invaded a kingdom, he
demanded that the king should send one of

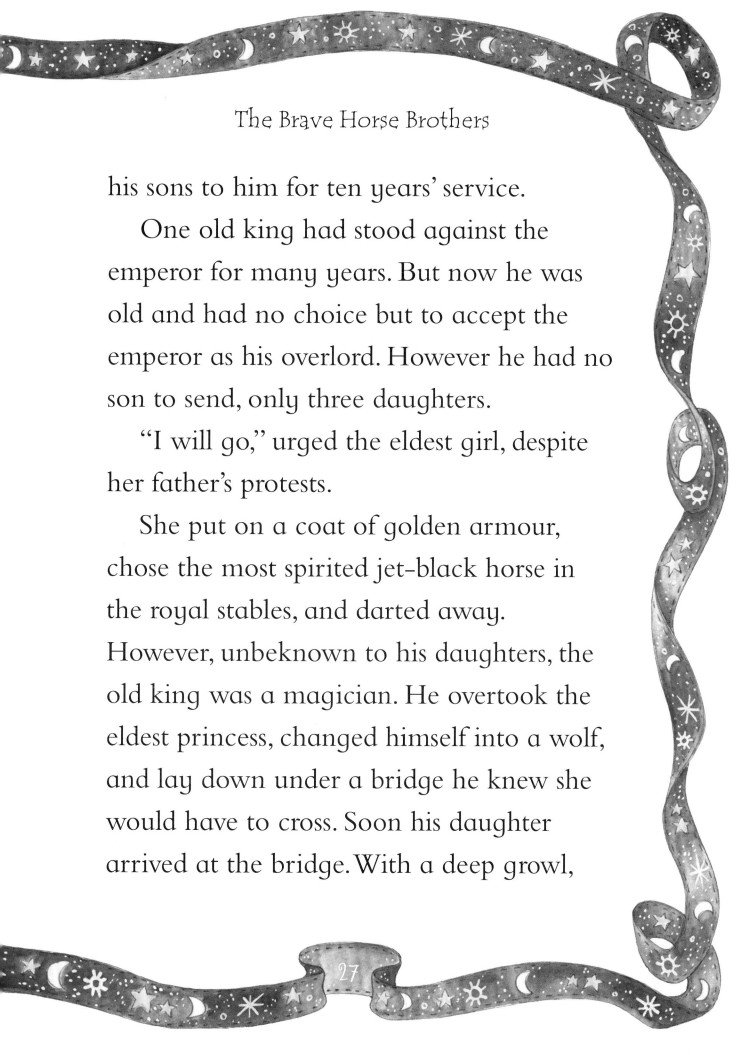

his sons to him for ten years' service.

One old king had stood against the emperor for many years. But now he was old and had no choice but to accept the emperor as his overlord. However he had no son to send, only three daughters.

"I will go," urged the eldest girl, despite her father's protests.

She put on a coat of golden armour, chose the most spirited jet-black horse in the royal stables, and darted away. However, unbeknown to his daughters, the old king was a magician. He overtook the eldest princess, changed himself into a wolf, and lay down under a bridge he knew she would have to cross. Soon his daughter arrived at the bridge. With a deep growl,

the wolf sprang up in front of the princess. The wolf was so terrifying that she turned her horse around and galloped home.

The very next day, the second princess begged to go. She donned gleaming silver armour and chose a prancing white stallion. But although she was prepared for the appearance of the wolf when she reached the bridge, she too was terrified and galloped home.

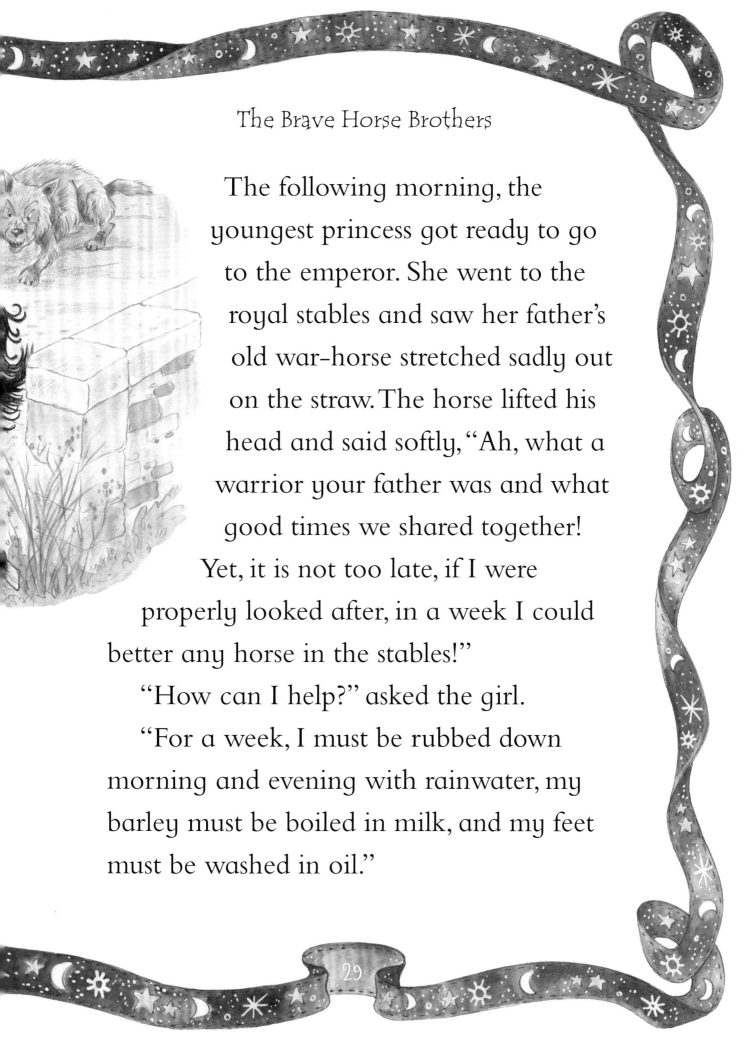

The following morning, the youngest princess got ready to go to the emperor. She went to the royal stables and saw her father's old war-horse stretched sadly out on the straw. The horse lifted his head and said softly, "Ah, what a warrior your father was and what good times we shared together! Yet, it is not too late, if I were properly looked after, in a week I could better any horse in the stables!"

"How can I help?" asked the girl.

"For a week, I must be rubbed down morning and evening with rainwater, my barley must be boiled in milk, and my feet must be washed in oil."

"I should like to try the treatment, as you might be able to help me."

"Try it then – you won't be sorry."

So the princess did as the horse had said. In a week's time its skin was shining like a mirror, its body was as fat as a watermelon and its movement as light as a deer.

Then, looking at the princess who had come early to the stable, the horse said joyfully, "May success always be yours, for you have given me back my life. I shall serve you as I served your father, if you will listen to what I say."

And so the delighted youngest daughter dressed in boy's clothes and rode away on the war-horse. A day's journey from the palace, she reached the bridge. But before they came in sight of it, the horse spoke soothing words and urged her not to be frightened. The huge wolf bounded howling towards her, but neither the horse nor the princess flinched. Instead, the princess bravely wielded her sword and the horse charged forwards across the bridge.

Once safely on the other side, the horse informed the princess that the wolf was really her own father! The girl didn't believe him – until the wolf changed back into her father before her very eyes.

The king flung his arms round her, saying, "Now I see that you are as brave as the bravest and as wise as the wisest, for you have chosen the right horse. With his help, you may reach the emperor and do well."

Then the princess received his blessing and they went their different ways.

The princess rode on until she came to the mountains that hold up the roof of the world. There she met two genies who had been fighting fiercely.

Seeing what they took to be a young man, one of the genies called out, "Deliver me from my enemy and I will give you a magic horn of power," while the other cried, "Help me to conquer this thief and you shall have my horse, Sunlight."

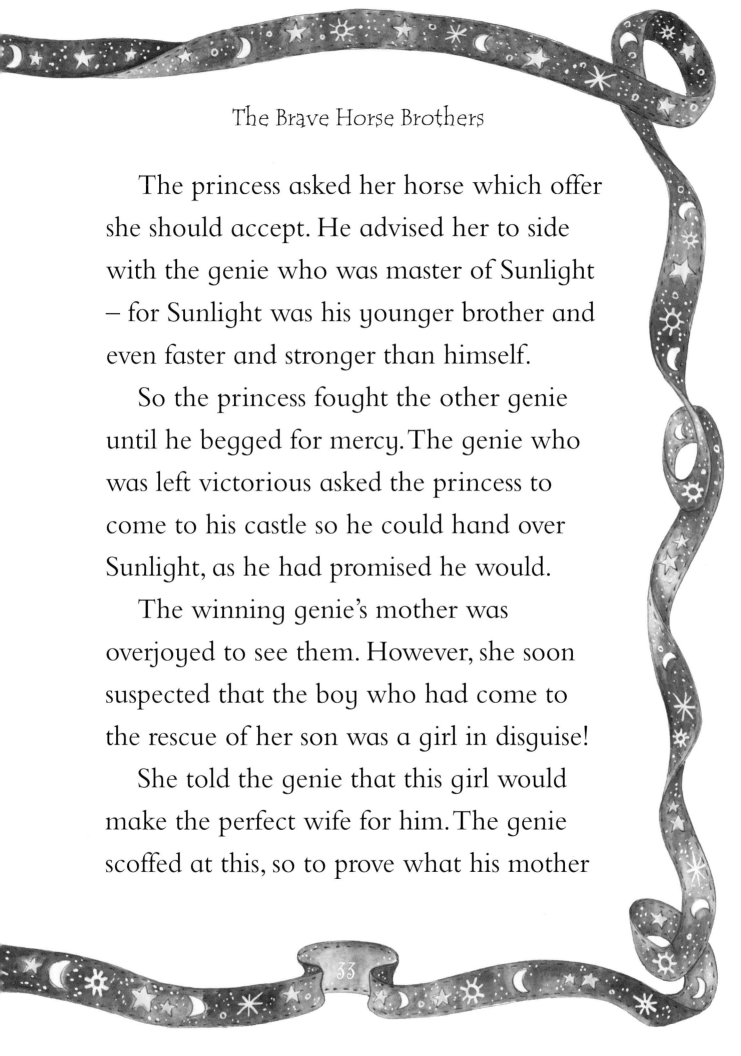

The princess asked her horse which offer she should accept. He advised her to side with the genie who was master of Sunlight – for Sunlight was his younger brother and even faster and stronger than himself.

So the princess fought the other genie until he begged for mercy. The genie who was left victorious asked the princess to come to his castle so he could hand over Sunlight, as he had promised he would.

The winning genie's mother was overjoyed to see them. However, she soon suspected that the boy who had come to the rescue of her son was a girl in disguise!

She told the genie that this girl would make the perfect wife for him. The genie scoffed at this, so to prove what his mother had said, at night, she laid on each of their pillows a handful of magic flowers that fade at the touch of a man, but remain eternally fresh in the fingers of a woman. Luckily, the clever horse had warned the princess what to expect. So when the house was silent, she crept softly to the genie's room and exchanged his faded flowers for hers.

In the morning, the old woman ran to see her son and found, as she knew she would, a bunch of dead flowers in his hand. But when she came to the bedside of the still-sleeping princess, she was astonished to see her also grasping withered flowers. There was nothing the mother could do!

When the princess awoke, she rode off with the two horses, but before they had got

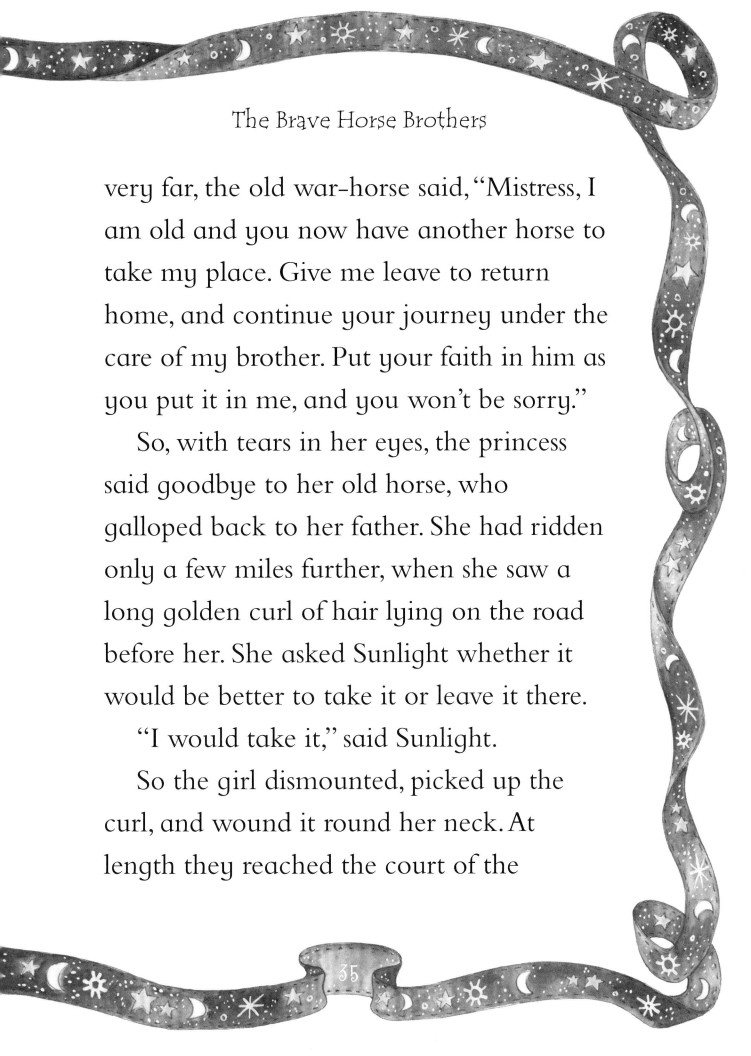

very far, the old war-horse said, "Mistress, I am old and you now have another horse to take my place. Give me leave to return home, and continue your journey under the care of my brother. Put your faith in him as you put it in me, and you won't be sorry."

So, with tears in her eyes, the princess said goodbye to her old horse, who galloped back to her father. She had ridden only a few miles further, when she saw a long golden curl of hair lying on the road before her. She asked Sunlight whether it would be better to take it or leave it there.

"I would take it," said Sunlight.

So the girl dismounted, picked up the curl, and wound it round her neck. At length they reached the court of the emperor. He was sitting on his throne, surrounded by the sons of the other kings, who served him as pages. The princess explained why she had come and the emperor received her kindly, declaring himself fortunate at finding a new page that was so brave, but also so charming.

From that moment on, the princess was the emperor's new favourite. The other pages soon grew jealous, and when they saw the golden curl around her neck they thought up a wicked plan to get rid of the new prince. They told the emperor that their new companion knew where the beautiful lost princess, Iliane, was to be found – and that he had a curl of her hair in his possession. The emperor was furious!

"Why did you tell me you knew the golden-haired Iliane? Unless you bring me the owner of this lock of hair, I will have your head cut off. Now go!"

Bowing low, the princess sadly left his presence and went to consult Sunlight. But at the horse's first words she brightened up – Sunlight had a plan!

"Do not be afraid, mistress, it is indeed Iliane's hair that you picked up on the road. A genie took her to a far-off island. Go back to the emperor and ask him for twenty ships filled with precious merchandise with which to tempt Iliane on board."

The ships were soon ready and the youngest princess entered the largest and finest, with Sunlight at her side. Then the sails were spread and the voyage began.

For seven weeks the wind blew them straight towards the west, until early one morning they caught sight of the island.

They cast anchor in a little bay and the princess disembarked with Sunlight. She tied a pair of tiny gold slippers to her belt, as the horse advised her to do. Then, mounting Sunlight, she rode until she met three servants. Their greedy eyes were caught by the glistening gold of the slippers and they hastened to their mistress to tell her of the arrival of the ships. Luckily the genie was away, so for the moment Iliane was free and alone. The servants described the slippers to her so well that she insisted on going to see them for herself.

They were even lovelier than she expected and so when the youngest princess begged Iliane to come onto the ships and inspect the other merchandise, Iliane's curiosity was too great to refuse.

Once she was onboard the ships sailed swiftly back to the court of the emperor. Iliane was treated with great respect by the emperor, who fell in love with her at first sight.

But though the emperor was satisfied, Iliane was not. She made a secret sign to Sunlight, who took a deep breath, then from one nostril breathed fresh air all over the youngest princess. To her surprise she was turned into a prince! From the other nostril the horse snorted a burning wind over the emperor, and all that was left of him was a pile of ash. Then Iliane turned to the prince and said, "It is you that saved me from the genie. I wish to marry you."

"Yes, I wish to marry you too," said the young prince, with a smile.